QUICKREADS

THE EXPERIMENT

ANNE SCHRAFF

QUICKREADS

SERIES 1
- Black Widow Beauty
- Danger on Ice
- Empty Eyes
- **The Experiment**
- The Kula'i Street Knights
- The Mystery Quilt
- No Way to Run
- The Ritual
- The 75-Cent Son
- The Very Bad Dream

SERIES 2
- The Accuser
- Ben Cody's Treasure
- Blackout
- The Eye of the Hurricane
- The House on the Hill
- Look to the Light
- Ring of Fear
- The Tiger Lily Code
- Tug-of-War
- The White Room

SERIES 3
- The Bad Luck Play
- Breaking Point
- Death Grip
- Fat Boy
- No Exit
- No Place Like Home
- The Plot
- Something Dreadful Down Below
- Sounds of Terror
- The Woman Who Loved a Ghost

SERIES 4
- The Barge Ghost
- Beasts
- Blood and Basketball
- Bus 99
- The Dark Lady
- Dimes to Dollars
- Read My Lips
- Ruby's Terrible Secret
- Student Bodies
- Tough Girl

ISBN-13: 978-1-61651-181-4
ISBN-10: 1-61651-181-8
eBook: 978-1-60291-903-7

Printed in Guangzhou, China
0311/03-150-11

15 14 13 12 11   2 3 4 5 6

■ ■ ■

"Mr. Ramos!" The psychology professor's voice startled Claudio as he sat before the computer.

"Oh, hi, Mr. Fruder," Claudio said. Odin Fruder was standing behind him in the empty computer lab. The man's tall, angular frame loomed like a bent, leafless tree. Claudio didn't like him. He wished he didn't need the money he earned as the professor's assistant.

"I see you're here very early today, Mr. Ramos," the professor said. "I like that. You're a dutiful fellow!"

"Yeah, I'm doing research for a project," Claudio said. "I don't get much time to keep up with homework, what with my part-time job. And it's like a three-ring circus at home. I've got three noisy little brothers, you know."

Mr. Fruder smiled. He had a very large mouth and several gleaming gold teeth. Somehow his smile reminded Claudio of an alligator's smirk. Although Claudio really had nothing against the teacher, the man just looked sinister. "You have a hard time, don't you, Mr. Ramos?" he asked in a smooth and oily voice. "You struggle to make ends meet. It's a real challenge for your family to stay afloat, eh?"

"Yeah," Claudio admitted, wondering what this was all about.

"Mr. Ramos, you are a very bright student. I would like you to do a special project for me. There would be additional pay, of course. But best of all, the project will be *interesting.*" Mr. Fruder's small, reptilian eyes gleamed. "You see, I'm doing a very important research paper on how various people react to fearful situations. Your part is simple. I want you to take several students out to a cavern. Once you get there you'll pretend to be trapped for a few hours. And you'll make note of the other students' behavior—"

Claudio was shocked. "That sounds—uh—really wild," he said nervously. How could he dupe his friends into being Fruder's unwitting guinea pigs?

"Your pay for the job would be excellent," Mr. Fruder said. "How much does your after-school job at that burger joint pay?"

"Uh—you know—minimum wage. Maybe a couple hundred bucks a month for part-time," Claudio said.

"For just one morning's work, I am offering a thousand dollars," Mr. Fruder said with a sly grin. He removed a thousand-dollar bill from his wallet. Then he wiggled it under Claudio's nose. He looked like a fisherman dangling a worm in front of a hungry fish!

A thousand dollars? Claudio felt weak. The whole room seemed to dance.

■ ■ ■

"So, what's this all about again?" Claudio asked. "I mean—it's not dangerous or anything, is it?"

Mr. Fruder settled his long body into a desk beside Claudio. "It's child's play. All you need to do is take three of your fellow students to this cavern." He took a map from his briefcase. "The directions are here. After you lead them deep inside, there will be a fake landslide and a giant boulder will block your escape."

"Huh? A landslide?" Claudio groaned. "That sounds risky."

"No, no, no! I'll send a fellow out there with a forklift. He'll simply drop a big boulder in front of the cavern entrance. It will make a loud noise, and you will cry, 'Oh! A landslide! We're trapped!' " The gold teeth in Mr. Fruder's mouth seemed to glitter with delight. "For the next few hours, your fellow students will scramble about, looking in vain for an escape—and *you* will jot down their reactions for my research paper. The forklift guy will hurry back to shove the boulder aside. He'll pretend that he heard the landslide and came to help. Then *voilà*—you will be rescued! And *you* will be a thousand dollars richer!"

The idea of easy money sounded good to Claudio. Dad's wages as a clerk in a convenience store weren't that good. And even when Mom worked part-time there was never enough money.

Claudio figured he could help at home, buy himself a few things, and then throw a nice party for his friends to make up for putting them through the ordeal. Of course, they would never know what really had happened.

"I guess I could do it," Claudio said.

"Excellent. We shall plan it for Wednesday. Tell your fellow students that it's a field trip. Say that they're supposed to find prehistoric cave paintings that reveal the emotional level of the cave folk," Mr. Fruder said.

"So, should I just pick any three kids?" Claudio asked.

"No—no indeed. I've already done that. Ask Ben Dunlap, Spike Hawley, and Dede Keene. I chose them carefully for the *types* of people they represent," Mr. Fruder said.

Although he knew them all, Claudio was glad that none of the three was a close friend. They were all in Mr. Fruder's psychology class. Ben was smart. He could even catch mistakes that teachers sometimes made. Spike was a clown and a wise guy who enjoyed disrupting class. Dede flirted a lot, but nobody could get a date with her. She liked to tease. At lunchtime, all three of them loved to sit around dissing teachers. Their jokes were actually pretty funny. Claudio had to admit that he, too, often joined in.

A thousand dollars! "Okay, Mr. Fruder, I guess it's a deal," Claudio said, trying to smile.

■ ■ ■

Claudio met with the three students on Tuesday. He wasn't proud of what he was doing. But he really needed the money. And nobody was going to get hurt, so what was the harm?

"Listen," Claudio said, "Mr. Fruder wants four of us to go to this cavern in the Chocolate Mountains to look for prehistoric cave paintings. We'll all get 350 grade points just for participating. And on Saturday I'm throwing a pizza party for all of us."

"So what are *you* getting out of it, man?" Ben asked curiously. "I don't need the 350 points. I already got an A in old Fruder's stupid class."

"Well, you know I'm Mr. Fruder's teaching assistant. He expects me to organize this kind of thing—as part of my job," Claudio said.

"*I* could use 350 points," Spike said. "That'd jump me up to a 'B' for sure."

"I could use the points, too," Dede

admitted, “but aren’t there bats in those caverns?”

“Nah,” Claudio said, turning to Ben. “If you go along, Ben, Mr. Fruder will mention all of our names in his important research paper. That’ll look good on your college applications.”

Ben nodded. “Yeah, I suppose that makes sense. How long will it take?”

“Just a couple hours. I’ll pick you all up in my van at eight in the morning. We shouldn’t be in the cavern more than thirty minutes—just long enough to scope out the paintings,” Claudio said. He was feeling guiltier than he thought he would. He’d never pulled such a stunt before. He felt like a rat. But he kept reminding himself that nobody was going to be the worse for it.

“Well, why not?” Ben said. “Might as well humor the old fool. Fruder looks just like Frankenstein’s monster—have you noticed? I stuck a movie poster of the monster on his bulletin board last week. When he saw it, I just about died laughing at the look on his face.”

Dede giggled. "I bet Fruder was ugly even when he was our age," she said.

Spike laughed, too. "Can you just imagine him as a teenager? I bet he had more zits than a garbage pail has flies!"

Everybody roared at that. Claudio laughed, too. He never started any of the ridicule against Mr. Fruder—but he *never* tried to stop it, either. Right now he had too much on his mind to worry about how the weird old teacher was losing the respect of his class.

■ ■ ■

Claudio got together some tape recorders and notebooks for the project. The night before he'd also gotten further instructions from Odin Fruder. One more time Mr. Fruder had told him not to worry. The party would be trapped in the cavern no longer than two hours at the most. Then they would all be rescued by the man driving the forklift.

Claudio picked up Spike first.

"Are we supposed to take notes or something?" Spike asked.

"I've got a notebook," Claudio said, fighting back another attack of guilty conscience. "I'll take all the notes."

"Great," Spike said. "I hate taking notes. It's so boring. I'd much rather be kicking a football around."

Then they picked up Dede and finally Ben. Ben wondered aloud if Mr. Fruder was doing this project in a last, desperate bid to save his job. "He really got blasted the last time students evaluated the teachers. Nearly all his students said he was a dud," Ben said.

"I sure told them he was the worst teacher I ever had," Dede said.

"Me, too," Spike agreed.

Claudio remembered the question sheet that had gone around to all the students. *"Ay Caramba!"* Claudio's dad had cried. "Kids should not pass judgment on their teachers!" But that's what had happened. Claudio had rated Mr. Fruder as a very poor teacher, too.

The hills grew steeper as they drove on. When he was in middle school, Claudio's scout troop had gone camping somewhere in this area. But he'd never been *in* the cavern.

Claudio glanced at the map Mr. Fruder had given him. Then he veered off on a narrow dirt road. "The instructions say to turn right at a cluster of junipers," he told the others.

In another half hour, they reached the cavern. Its mouth looked like nothing more than a small hole in the side of a mountain.

"I can't imagine there are really cave paintings in there," Ben scoffed.

"Yeah, old Frankenstein's monster must be dreaming," Dede laughed.

Claudio parked near the entrance, his jaw set grimly. He was really uncomfortable about this. But it was too late to turn back now. In his mind, he had already spent that thousand dollars. Help for Mom and Dad, his schoolbooks, maybe enough money to take that pretty girl at the burger joint, Alita Gonzalez, to the movies a few times.

"Let's go," Claudio said, leading the way into the cavern. He didn't dare delay for fear that he'd change his mind and call the whole thing off.

"Ewww!" Dede cried when she threw her flashlight beam at the ceiling. "Look, you guys! Zillions of hideous bats are hanging up there!"

Ben laughed. "Don't worry. We'll be long gone before they wake up—right, Claudio?"

"Yeah, Ben, that's right," Claudio said in a faint voice.

■ ■ ■

"I don't see any cave paintings," Ben snorted as he swept the walls of the cavern with his flashlight beam.

"We've got to go deeper," Claudio said. "According to the map Mr. Fruder gave me, there's another room up ahead." After a few minutes Claudio's legs felt like they weren't doing a very good job of holding him up. He was nervously waiting for the other shoe to drop—for the forklift guy to arrive and drop the boulder over the entrance to the cave.

Claudio didn't have to wait long.

Spike was the one who let out the loudest yell when the boulder crashed against the entrance. *"It's a quake, you guys!"* he screamed.

Ben shouted, "Come on, let's get out of here! Just before the quake I thought I heard an engine. I think there's a guy in a truck out there!"

Dede reached the entrance first. She screamed, "It's closed in! Our way out is gone! Oh, no!"

Claudio was sick to his stomach with guilt. What kind of a monster put other people through misery like this for a lousy thousand bucks? He hated himself. He wished he could reverse the whole deal—but it was too late!

"Help!" Ben yelled. "I *know* I heard a truck out there! Come on, you guys, let's all holler for help so he can hear us!"

They got up a frantic chorus of screams and shouts for help. Even Claudio—who knew where that engine noise had come from—joined in. The forklift driver who had dropped the boulder was not in any big hurry to help them. But only he knew that.

"The engine sound is fainter. It's like he's going away," Spike groaned.

"He's trying to save his own dirty hide," Ben grumbled bitterly. "There's probably a lot of damage out there from the quake."

As Claudio stared at the distraught faces of the three students, he felt like vomiting. Ben's face was ashen, Spike was paralyzed by terror, and Dede was trembling and crying like a baby.

Mr. Fruder's instructions came back to Claudio now: *As your fellow students vainly scramble about looking for an escape, be sure to jot down their reactions for my research paper.*

Claudio didn't even try to follow those instructions. He was numb with remorse and disgust at himself. He wouldn't make it worse by taking notes! He didn't care about the thousand dollars anymore. In a way, it was blood money. To deliberately frighten people like this *had* to be a crime.

Claudio felt like a criminal. The only thing that kept him sane was knowing that the forklift operator would return before long.

■ ■ ■

There's gotta be some way for us to move that boulder," Ben said. "We have to use our brains."

Spike pushed against the rocky barrier with his shoulder. "Man, this sucker must weigh *tons!"* he groaned. "No way we're going to budge it!"

"Maybe there's another way out," Dede said in a small, shaky voice. "We haven't explored the whole cave yet. It could be there's another entrance."

Ben suddenly turned to Claudio. There was a suspicious look on his face— at least it looked that way to Claudio. "Hey, how come you're so quiet, genius? After all, it's all your fault that we're in this mess. So how about *you* come up with some ideas, okay?"

"It didn't seem like a big deal," Claudio

mumbled. "Just—you know—a field trip." The others didn't know what Claudio had done, of course. But *he* knew, and now he was afraid that they were onto him.

"How come you're working with that old creep anyway?" Ben demanded. "You must be the teacher's pet, right?"

"Look, you guys, I need the money he pays for me to be a teacher's assistant. And hey—I didn't *force* anyone into this," Claudio argued nervously.

"No, but you dangled all those grade points under our noses. How could we resist?" Dede complained bitterly.

They were all turning on him, and they didn't know the half of it! Claudio tried to think fast. "Hey, you know that engine we heard? I bet that guy has gone for help. That must be why he drove off so fast." Claudio glanced at his watch. They'd been trapped for almost 20 minutes. It might be a long time before the forklift guy would return for the rescue. As ugly as the trio was turning, Claudio dreaded what was ahead.

"I say we get busy looking for another way out," Ben said.

"Yeah," Dede agreed, glad that her idea was at last flying. "Come on. There could be a little crevice somewhere just big enough for us to get through."

Ben led the way deeper into the cavern. Before every step he swept the flashlight beam before them.

"Look, there's a passageway over there," Ben said excitedly.

"It doesn't look wide enough for a person to walk through even sideways," Spike said.

Ben and Spike turned to Dede. "You're the smallest one of us. You have to try to get through, Dede," Ben said.

"Yeah, right! *I* should get wedged in some slimy passageway," Dede groaned.

"You gotta do it, girl," Spike said. "You might be able to squeeze right out of the cave. Then you could go for help."

Dede stared at the damp walls of the passageway. She let out a little screech. "Look! Some kind of hideous pale bugs are all over the walls. . . they'll crawl all over me!" she cried.

■ ■ ■

Dede, don't be chicken!" Spike scolded. "If we don't get out of here, we'll die. We gotta do our best to escape!"

"Come on, you guys," Claudio argued nervously. "Why are you panicking so quickly? That engine we heard—I'm sure it was a guy going for help. Can't we just be patient for a while and try to keep our heads?"

Ben whirled around and turned the full light of the flashlight beam on Claudio's face. "How can you be so sure? Huh? Huh?" He reached out and grabbed Claudio's shirtfront. "What do you know that we don't know, man? Something fishy is going down here. We're all scared to death, and you're *way* too cool. You and Fruder got some scheme going? Huh? Huh?" He gave Claudio a hard shake.

"Nothing's going down," Claudio gasped. "You guys all heard that engine out there. It *had* to be somebody who knows we're in trouble. He'll send help!"

"I wonder," Ben said grimly, the hostility growing on his face. "I'm not sure there *was* an earthquake. And if there wasn't, then how did that boulder get in front of the entrance?"

Spike joined Ben in confronting Claudio. Claudio winced. Spike was a lot more frightening than Ben. Ben was just average in size, but Spike was huge—a heavyweight wrestler. Claudio had seen the look of brutal glee on his face when he'd get some other guy in a death grip.

"Old Fruder always did seem to like you, Ramos," Spike said. "You're the *only* one he seems to like. Maybe you and Fruder planned this whole thing."

"You're crazy," Claudio cried, his voice trembling. "What for? Why would I? I don't like Fruder either. I gave him a poor rating just like everybody else. I blasted him, too—and laughed at him!"

Dede joined in the attack. "Since Claudio and Fruder planned this, Claudio must know about some escape hatch. I bet that the minute we turn our backs, he'll be out of here!"

Spike moved directly in front of Claudio. He grabbed a handful of Claudio's shirt and brought his classmate's perspiring face up close to his. "You got a real nice face, Ramos. I know a little dark-haired chick at the burger joint who's crazy about you. What do you think? When I bust your face open and spread your nose all over your cheeks—will she still think you're good-looking?" he snarled.

"Wait, you guys—you're all wrong," Claudio stammered. He was drenched in perspiration. Any fool could see that he was lying through his teeth.

"You give up the truth, man—and do it *now!*" Ben warned.

Claudio's heart was pounding like a jackhammer.

"Okay, okay," Claudio cried. "It was all ajoke! But we'll all get out of here in forty minutes! We aren't in any danger—I promise! It was just a dumb joke that Fruder thought up!"

■ ■ ■

Spike shook Claudio the way a cat shakes a mouse. "Nah, that's not the whole story. Give us the *whole* story. Fruder's not a joker, man."

"Okay," Claudio said. "It was an experiment. Fruder is writing a paper. He wanted me to write notes about how fear affected you guys when you thought you were trapped in the cavern. There wasn't any quake. A guy with a forklift shoved the boulder in front of the cavern. Don't worry. The same guy is coming back to push it away any minute now."

"You dirty little creep!" Dede cried shrilly. "You agreed to trap us and make us think we were maybe dying? Then you were going to write down how we were acting?"

"Why'd you do it, man?" Ben asked in disbelief.

"He was—uh—he was going to give me a thousand dollars, and my family needs the money and, you know, you guys were gonna get better grades and I was gonna throw a big pizza party afterwards. I didn't think anybody would be hurt—" Claudio hoped for a little sympathy, but he saw nothing but hatred in the faces that stared at him.

"Listen, you guys," Claudio pleaded, "I'm really sorry. I regretted it right away. I didn't even *start* taking notes or recording anything like he wanted me to. I felt terrible about it."

Ben strode over to the corner and started rummaging through Claudio's backpack. "Yeah, look at the notebooks and the tape recorders he was gonna use. He was actually gonna *record* our misery and make it public. The rotten little creep sold us out!" Ben said.

Dede was looking in the backpack, too. She pulled out an envelope stuck in one of the notebooks. "Look, guys—it's addressed to Claudio from Fruder!"

Ben ripped the envelope open.

Claudio didn't even know that Fruder had written him a letter. As far as he knew, Fruder had already given him all his instructions. Now Dede shone her flashlight beam on the neatly printed letter and read it aloud.

Claudio: Go to the first small room and find an indentation in the west wall. You will see a cassette player. Listen to the cassette I placed there last week. Odin Fruder.

Dede quickly found the cassette player and hit the play button.

"My dear students who hate me so much," came the nasal voice of Odin Fruder, "when you hear this you will be trapped in a remote mountain cavern. By now, a terrible sense of doom must be settling in your souls. You know—don't you—that the shadow of death is hovering over you?"

■ ■ ■

Claudio listened to the tape with horror. What was going on? This wasn't what was supposed to be happening. This wasn't part of the plan.

The professor's voice droned on:

"Dede Keene, you have tormented me in class for the final time with your sly insults and disruptive humor. Spike Hawley, you

are a vile brute. Because of pressure from the football coach, I was forced to give you better grades than you deserved. Ben Dunlap, you twit, how you enjoyed humiliating me when I made a small error! But I reserve for Claudio Ramos my deepest hatred. Although I gave you a job, you always joined the others in undermining me. And just as you betrayed me, so now I betray you. I shall be terminated at the end of the school year. Thanks to you, my career—which is all I live for—will be over. I close with the name you so delighted in giving me: Yours very truly, Frankenstein's Monster."

"There's no forklift coming to remove that boulder! We'll never get out!" Ben cried. "He means for us to die here!"

Spike turned to Claudio. In his rage, Spike started to shake him violently. "*You* did this to us! *You* did it!"

"But I never suspected that he'd do anything like this!" Claudio gasped.

"I'm gonna smash you," Spike said, drawing back his hammy fist.

"*No!*" Ben yelled, dragging Spike off

Claudio. "We need everybody to get us out of here! We'll deal with him later."

"You're going to crawl through the passageway, Ramos," Ben said then. "Dede is afraid. So you're going. You will probably get stuck—but you've got a chance, because you're skinnier than Spike and me. If you like living, man, you'd better try real hard!"

Claudio didn't argue. He stripped off his sweatshirt and started into the passageway.

Moving sideways, he inched along slowly. He felt the limestone ripping his T-shirt. Then he felt the blood come.

"The passageway seems to be getting narrower," Claudio shouted. "I don't think I can go much farther."

Spike shouted, *"Keep going!* If you come back without making any headway, you're dead meat, Ramos."

Claudio felt a sharp outcropping of rock cut his back. But he forced himself farther along until the passageway widened a little. Then Claudio popped out in another small room! High up on one wall he could see a gaping hole. It might be large enough to get through! But it was at least 15 feet straight up. Claudio looked around frantically.

He saw a vertical rock formation rising like a candle from the floor. Could he climb it? As he worked his way up, a sharp, lime-encrusted rock gouged his arm, and he almost fell. But slowly, slowly he clawed his way up toward the hole.

■ ■ ■

With bloody fingers Claudio grabbed for the rim of the hole and dragged himself up toward the light. Suddenly, he saw blue sky! In a moment he scrambled up and out of the cavern. His heart pounded with relief as he worked his way down the rocks toward where he had left his van.

But the van was gone. Claudio saw that the forklift had pushed the van into a ravine. It lay there in a crumpled wreck. *Of course* Fruder wouldn't leave a van parked nearby! Not when he intended the cavern to be a tomb for his enemies. Sooner or later the van would have attracted attention.

Claudio went to the boulder that blocked the cave and yelled, "I'm out! They've wrecked the van, but I'm going for help. Just hang in there. I'll be back!"

"That's another lie, Ramos!" Spike screamed. "You're getting away yourself and leaving us to rot here!"

"You creep!" Ben yelled.

"How *could* you, Claudio! You don't deserve to live," Dede sobbed.

Claudio tried to ignore their hurtful insults so he could concentrate on finding help. Just before they had turned onto the dirt road, he remembered seeing a little yellow farmhouse. So now Claudio started running fast. His legs ached and his breath came in hard, painful rasps, but he ran on. He ignored the pounding in his chest and the numbness in his limbs as he forced himself to keep going.

When he finally saw the house, Claudio staggered onto the porch and screamed, "Call—the—police!"

When the police came, Claudio told his story. Within the hour there was a forklift at the cavern, shoving the giant rock out of the way. At about the same time, Odin Fruder was captured at the airport as he was trying to book a flight to Austria.

The police gave the four college students a ride to their homes. As they rode along in silence, Ben turned to Claudio and said, "Hey, creep, when are you having the pizza party?"

"Yeah, and I want extra toppings on mine," Spike said.

"After what you did, it better be the best pizza we ever ate!" Dede said.

A grateful smile trembled on Claudio's lips. He didn't know how he could afford a pizza party. But he knew he would find the money somehow—even if he had to hock everything he owned.

Maybe these guys would be able to forgive him after all. And if they did, maybe someday Claudio could forgive himself.

After-Reading Wrap-Up

1. Would you trust Claudio? Would you want him as a friend? Why or why not?

2. Do you feel sorry for Claudio? Give your reasons.

3. When you learned that Fruder never intended to rescue the students, were you surprised? Explain your answer.

4. Suppose Fruder *hadn't* intended to murder students. Would Claudio have felt guilty anyway? Support your answer by quoting the story.

5. Which character in *The Experiment* was most like you? Which was least like you? Write two short paragraphs explaining your answer.